Massimiliano Sassoli de Bianchi

Fragments
of a rebirth

Memories, visions and
impressions in search
of the inner being

Original title: Frammenti di una rinascita
Title: Fragments of a rebirth
Author: Massimiliano Sassoli de Bianchi
Translation from Italian: Stewart and Maria Bryant
Cover: Paola Patocchi

- *First Edition* -

www.massimilianosassolidebianchi.ch

ISBN: 978-1-4466-6426-1

Published by: Lulu (www.lulu.com)

Index

Preface

7

Fragments

13

Preface

I wrote this text with the purpose of integrating into one account some fragments of my life and transform them into something new.

Fragments that are mostly interior, made of memories, fantasies, fantasying, visions, meetings, reflections, impressions, feelings, emotions…

I wrote all this offhand, without a

predetermined structure.

I didn't know where I was starting or where it would end. The text almost composed itself.

It was an unfolding of my mind with a logic that I would discover only at the end of the story. I was writer and spectator at the same time.

When I understood that the hand didn't want to continue anymore, that there weren't any more fragments to metabolize, just as it started the story finished.

Rereading it, I felt a deep emotion. I was touched by how my inner being was made naked and seen in its entireness, maybe for the first time.

For many days, I reread it several times. I wanted to nourish myself as much as possible from this new vibration, whose transforming power was impressed in the story.

In each rereading, a part of me resounded in a new way with the wholeness of my being. It was like going on a search of pieces that had been asleep in me, to awaken them and add them into a puzzle of which I don't know the final count of pieces.

I shared the story with other people.

I understood that anybody could receive something from its reading. In fact, there are many common elements of our unconscious: symbols, archetypes, images, signs, sounds, impressions, that pertain to a unique human experience, typical to all men and women.

Widely sharable.

Fragments

In a house by the edge of a lake, there lived a man. A man who spent his days looking at the sky. A man whose soul was always that of a child.

The roof of his house seemed to play with the roofs of his neighbors houses, like in a mysterious forest. He often thought of his true home, but didn't know where to look for it.

So he dreamed. He dreamed of the

immense sky and the timid and majestic stars. At that time of dreaming, gently, he began to remember… when he was still a baby in the great mothers' womb.

Who was that child? He didn't know. His memories got lost between roofs and sky. Exiled refugees in no man's land, at impossible borders between irreconcilable worlds.

A glass of wine at times helps, I thought. It warms the heart and helps to live. Only at times though. Who was that child? Who was he?

It's dark. My breath moves in the womb of the great mother. In the womb of mother earth. Then from the earth to the mother. The womb of the mother.

It's nice. It's not too cold. I speak to her, but she does not answer. I despair. Isn't there anybody here with me? I'm afraid.

There it is, now she's moving. But she's not moving with me. What am I doing here? Where is the sky? Where are the beloved stars?

If I don't feed myself I'll die. I decide to feed myself. I eat, but I don't feel the warmth.

Where are you my father? Where are you my mother? Where is your warm hug? Everything is so neutral, impersonal. Will it be the same later? Who will be there to welcome me?

I'm not sure if I want to come out. But it is necessary. So I decided. Decided… but when? I'm already forgetting. Forgetting the stars. Forgetting the sky.

It's time to be born. Courage. Yes, courage, I will need it. Now there's no turning back.

It's done! As I thought. It's cold. Everything's so cold. I hear voices, but I don't recognize them.

I pour a little more wine. I need some. It helps me. I look at the roofs. They are strange hats. In my house at the edge of the lake, I think and dream. Dream and think. I light a cigarette. The smoke drifts silently and up towards the sky.

I forgot how much I missed the sky. But there is life. There is the struggle. There is everything that I wanted. Now it's too late to go back.

I am a strong trunk. Nothing can scratch my thick bark. Nothing can pull out my thick roots. I was born to withstand. I was born to bring my solid arms to the sky and shout! Yes, shout!

Did I shout when I came out of that womb? I don't remember. I imagine that I did.

The imagination can be dangerous and at the same time a blessing. What would we be without it? How can we fill up all those holes? How can we survive?

But it cannot last forever. We need to learn how to fill the holes with the truth.

The truth…

I find myself in a cave, dark and a bit humid. At the end of the cave are two wide openings. Two passages. I can catch a glimpse of the sun reflecting its morbid rays on the sea. Those openings are two eyes that observe me.

I am in the womb of the great mother. I feel good, but I want to run. To escape. I want to go through the two eyes. I run, I jump, I fly…

I pass through those two sockets and I am born again. I take my leap in search for freedom.

It won't be easy, I know.

Roofs on the houses and houses under the roofs. Houses that desire to open their roofs like big eyes to the sky.

I light up another cigarette. The smoke rises, as usual. It follows the draft. It travels towards the clouds and dissolves in the sun.

Beloved sun.

Now I am an android. A being maybe completely mechanical. But intelligent. He is me and I am him. He, the android, seems fine. Apparently fine. But what can that word even mean for him?

With coldness, slowly, he observes from his viewer. He is a sophisticated being, very powerful. There are no limits to what he is able to do.

He has no fear.

But he is not a true android. As strange as it may seem he desires! He desires that his viewer would be wider. He desires to see the sky.

Beloved sky.

He's been programmed for something. But for what? His noble behavior makes me believe that his power is for the service of humanity. But of which humanity? And what would be his power?

Now I notice his solitude. His profound and immense nostalgia.

I observe him… I observe myself.

His chest begins to pulsate red. His armor breaks. A body of a dry man comes out, freeze-dried, without life.

A dried out old stick.

The man, or what is left of him, falls rigidly to the earth. One thing is certain: he's been dead for a long time.

I pour another glass and put on some music. The chimneys on the roofs seem like antennas pointed towards the sky, and the antennas seem like chimneys from another world.

I want to cry, but I can’t.

So I smoke. The smoke rises. As it always rises. Then finally the tears come. The smoke rises and the water of life descends.

Now I am a little girl with blond hair and nice braids. I am full of life. She is smart. Very smart. As smart as the beauty of her long golden braids.

It seems that she is playing, but actually she is searching for something. Her look is like an endless deep well. Green and intense like an antique jade jewel.

She is Jade. She is me and I am her. She is searching and yet she knows. She knows and yet she is still searching.

A shot erases part of her sweet face. A crisp and sharp sound. An arrow that breaks on the young trunk of a flowering tree.

Her eyes have changed. Now they are more profound, unfathomable. They are the eyes of an enchantress, of a witch, of an alien entity. They are the eyes of a priestess. They have the color of knowledge. Sweet and elusive at the same time.

Something unthinkable has happened. Unhoped-for. The girl approaches the android, whose metallic body lies on the ground, broken in half. She takes the place of the man that was. She closes that metal giant on herself. She blends with him. As if they have always been one structure.

The android is transformed. He becomes less android and more of a girl. More human. Stronger. Bigger still. In the end, he becomes alive and sets himself free in the sky. He flies in conquest of endless space. He's born to be free. That was his program. That was his mission. Now he knows the secret of timeless power: Jade, the gem of the heart.

Will that girl grow? Will she know how to transform that ancient armor?

It’s worth it to try.

I smoke among the roofs that smoke.

I'm always thinking about him, the android. And I think about the girl, Jade, that entered his womb.

I need to descend to grow. The courage of that girl nourishes my soul. Will that also be my courage? The courage to be born again…

The courage to descend and then

ascend… to then redescend and again ascend… for how long?

The weight of the armor becomes unbearable. How much strength and power in that extraordinary structure. I am proud of it. But then humbly I ask myself: why all of this?

I search around for that strange little girl with the golden braids and with that far away look. Where has she gone?

I realize that she never left me. I am too big and she is too small. That's why we can't see each other. But our hearts almost touch each other.

We only have to touch lightly. Dare to touch.

I bravely ask her:

"Who are you?"

She responds:

"I am you and you are me. I am the life, the essence, the meaning."

Simple words, yet so true. So I confide:

"I'm afraid of life. I'm afraid of you. I want to hold your hand, but I'm afraid I'll hurt you.

She looks at me and her words are marvelous:

"Don't be afraid. You are already holding my hand, and I'm not afraid of you, because I love you."

It was true. My metallic hand rested upon hers.

I hugged her and her light body once again became one with mine.

Again I was born. But this time it was different. This time I didn't break.

I look at the windows that face mine. I think about many openings. About many caves. Birth, life, death. And then again birth. Androids and children of other houses. Other stories.

I always think about them. About the android and my sweet little girl. A distant memory pops up. So distant that the memory is like a dream and the dream is like a memory.

The android and the little girl look at me with a sweetness that scares me. I get lost in their powerful beings. In their immense life.

Their story begins and their voice is like a balm to my wounds. It's a timeless story that I have lived a thousand times. But never believed. A story of victories and defeats. Of innumerous battles, lived in valor, in the endless course of my existence. The story of a pain born of an ancient sacrifice, in the attempt to save what I held dearest.

I lived in a far away land, in time and in space. Where injustice and terror reigned. A place where law was not understood. In the shadow of that realm I fought to bring the light again. To light again that flame that was already burning in me.

"You carried the law and the sword at the same time."

Said the android and the girl with one voice.

“But you decided to lose them both, abandoning every trace of nobility that was within you. Of your noble lineage. Do you remember the pain? Do you remember the courage of that difficult choice?”

I tried, but I couldn’t remember:

“What choice?”

“Don’t you remember? You entered into a hard reality, barbarous and violent. Without any hope. You wanted to understand existence from inside, without the prejudice of a higher vision. You led the people in their journey towards the light. You made that journey again, together with them.

Today you are ready to remember that flame that is renewed in the beauty of your being. You are ready to remember the ancient pain. The pain of having forgotten. The pain of having had to abdicate to then reconquer.

Reconquer the ancient splendor.

It's the time of remembrance. You can unite again with your brothers. You can return home. Listen to our pain.

You are us and we are you.

We are the symbol of that noble and sovereign quality, which for so long was sacrificed to allow the blooming of an even more perfumed flower.

Let your perfume ravish you. Let our words enter you. Don't doubt. Trust in us. Because we are you and you are us.

There needs to be more wine.

Ancient battles and noble warriors. Fantasies, dreams, imaginations…

reality? Who am I?

I see a cloud of smoke coming out from a chimney. A waft of wind and the cloud dissolves. Did it really exist? I need to ask the wind.

I thought again of the warrior. I can still hear his voice:

"It's not necessary anymore to lose everything. The sacrifice has already been made. Now it's time to love, without suffering anymore!"

How right he is. My heart can open to the essence of the existence without my armor exploding. Without getting lost again.

Dear and sweet heart, I look at you and see you. You are swollen and I know why. You had so much love to give. But you were a prisoner. Prisoner of your own love. Prisoner of your own fear to love. So needy of that strength that you didn't know was already yours. So chained in your need of freedom.

I enter the armor of the android. I feel my heart beat. It beats so strong that its vermilion color penetrates through the thick metal. It warms it. It melts it. It opens it.

Sad destiny. To die a prisoner of a structure whose reason to be was to help me to live. That child is dead. But has never ceased to live in me.

Maybe he only built that armor as a game. But then wasn't able to get out of it. Or he got out, yes, but rigid and dried up like an old man of a thousand years.

But his heart didn't want to die. Hidden, in the darkness of that armor, he discovered how to continue to grow. To nourish himself. Until the completion of his escape.

No heart can bear the weight of chains for too long.

I shouted my desperation to heaven. I severed those chains offering them to God. All of my being vibrated and I fell to my knees, moved by a powerful healing energy.

For a moment, I believed that I would dematerialize.

The borders of the chains suspended in the emptiness and the angels of fire to disintegrate their links one by one.

That little boy is dead. Now he is a little girl with blond braids and a distant look. Hers is the strength that shows respect for the heart.

I will need to learn to love her. Help her to grow. Teach her to love. And when her young body will be mature, I will tell her how to explode in a fire of a thousand feelings.

She looks at me and says:

“I am virgin territory ready to be explored”.

It’s night. The ashes of my cigarette burn like a far away bonfire that rests in the womb of the great mother. Far away like my memories.

I try to run after them but they escape. As usual. How long have I been in that powerful armor? Very long… too long!

An apnea that lasted the breath of an infancy, flying away like a kite on its first test flight.

A sleep that lasted the fragment of an adolescence. Just touched on the surface. Never lived.

An illusion that lasted the length of a marriage and of two wonderful children.

And I'm always there, trying to perceive the world from the bottom of my mechanical covering. Observing it from my limited viewer.

Years lived in anesthesia.

I didn't have time to grow. I have always been big. An android doesn't grow. An android is born big. Programmed to be efficient. Not to grow.

Growing is a problem. Growing is a disease for the others that don't want to grow. And the others are always so dam strong.

Gigantic robots.

I smile and think of those sweet words that came to my aid. Like a rain that washes the wounds of an arid desert:

"Don't be afraid, don't be afraid. Your mistake was not made today, but then.

A choice without love!"

Now I understand in which halter I've run myself into. I went down a road that wasn't mine. A road that was forcefully suggested and that I, with a pure and sincere soul, followed without hesitation.

The trail was full of obstacles. Of difficulties. Of misunderstandings. But I was very talented. I built a metallic warrior in which I could hide myself and pretend to grow.

Then I discovered that that trail didn't belong to me. I discovered that I needed to put on a new garment. I needed… But I didn't feel supported. I was afraid not to be adequate for that garment. To fail trying.

I preferred to assume a role rather than listen to the reasons of my heart.

What a big mistake to not consider the

heart, the aspirations, life. But you can forgive a child.

Poor child. He chose non love forgetting the reasons of his feelings.

He chose non love to understand love. And that same feeling he suffocated has vindicated itself. Obscuring him. Suggesting that it was him at fault for not being able to give love.

So he exchanged being big with love. He confused protection with love. The assuming of responsibility with love.

It took so many years to understand. To feel again the call of his true nature, which showed other paths.

The voice returns to my aid:

"You can play around with everything but not with feelings. It's not important to affirm your own will, but to want what you love."

"I want to love!"

I shout. But the voice continues:

"What has been given to you needs to be acknowledged and given back. You are a man of peace. Your role is to find solutions. To build harmonies. To support… Your values, your consciousness, allows you all this. Don't be afraid."

I return to myself. I return to the present. I return to my omnipresent head. To my heavy shoulders. To my sad and sensitive heart. To my plexus which is tense… very tense.

I return to my shabby belly. To my tired legs. I'm not doing well. Where is that magnetic strength hiding that is able to unite, melt and reassemble?

Power.

I go to light another cigarette. But then I change my mind.

I sit in an Indian position on my carpet. The singing of a feminine voice, sweet and smooth, opens my heart and moves me.

Laughter ruins the poetry of that moment. All we needed was him: the witness!

He looks at me with despising superiority. He looks at the sad ballet of my parts. Foreign. Detached.

A blinding light explodes. A lightening. The witness finds himself nude.

Part among the parts.

Sweet illusion that of the parts, that makes us believe that we possess our own identity, separate from the rest of the cosmos.

Bitter illusion that of the parts, that limits us, denies us, fragments us. Kills us.

It hurts to be cut into pieces.

I look for a way out. I invent an infinite succession of witnesses. Strange Russian dolls. Then I ask myself:

"Who observes the observer?"

I don't know how to answer… I fail. But a new question is born:

"Who are you mysterious force that blows life into me?"

To hell with the witness! Sweet and powerful life that blows in me and permits me to exist. Powerful ray that with your strength sustains and nourishes the entire universe.

Love.

If I am a strong trunk, why is it all so difficult? Which misunderstanding would ever shake my base, my deep roots, my wide branches?

Why does the same law that gave me my radiance – ancient lighthouse in a sea at tempest – also brings me a sense of separation?

And with separation, pain.

Is separation the root of pain? Or the illusion that separation rhymes with division? You cannot unite what has always been divided. But it is possible to reassemble what has been only apparently separated.

Love.

This is the passageway for all of us. Little lights or powerful lighthouses. The difficult task for everyone is the passage to a dimension located in the heart.

You cannot stop the arrival of a big wave. No one can swim against its current, without the risk of drowning.

My dear android, now I understand the reasons for your very old armor. This passage I cannot complete it by sight, or hearing. But through feeling. Perceiving.

This skin which my naked body has dressed itself in, made me sensitive. Very sensitive.

Every time a shock!

And every shock another veil on my memory. Another layer on my armor, in the attempt to protect that vulnerable creature.

It's difficult to discover that not even nourishment from the mother is free. But requires submitting to multiple requirements.

It wasn't like that before being born. Before being born I had tasted of that love that was without price. Given without asking anything in return.

Down here it's not the same thing. Down here the word of order is to conform, to conform, to conform…

The more I conformed to that alien blackmail the more they loved me. So I created you, the android. Otherwise I would die.

My skin was too sensitive.

Do you remember papa's voice? Like a thunder. He was strong and I couldn't make it. I wanted to learn to be strong, but nobody taught me how to.

Every so often I wanted to cry. But not even that did they teach me how to do. I didn't know how to cry alone. And at least in that I wanted to be strong. At least I wanted to be good at that.

Androids don't cry, I thought. So I decided to become you. You warned me:

"Don't do it! The price to pay is too high. You won't feel anything under my armor. You can't grow anymore. Become strong. I will need to become strong in your place."

I silenced you:

"All the better! Now it's time to just survive."

But in the end you are dead, my little one. But to be born again as a young girl with golden braids, and mysterious eyes that look far away.

I take a deep breath.

I disgust cigarettes. I light up another one. The smoke enters and leaves. Contraction, expansion, contraction, expansion… the breath slows. The stomach dilates and calm enters in.

It's a strange therapy that of the smoker. He loves to breath. He smokes to breath. But while he smokes he kills his own breath. Don't we do this also in life? We love it deeply. Nothing is more important than it. But nobody taught us how to love it.

In our ignorance we have fallen into a tragic trap.

Do you want to live? Then kill! Kill all that you love. Deny it. Destroy it. Only in this way will you discover what life is.

We believed it. Because nothing was more important to us than to feel alive. We even ended up mistaking the cigarette for breathing. To the point of believing that only if we smoke are we able then to breath. Only by annihilating life we would be able to live.

But life doesn't care about our ignorance. Life is. Life just is. If we destroy it then it destroys us.

Because we are life.

If we deny life then life denies us. Because life loves us. In the good and in the bad.

Its love becomes then so intense, so urgent, that it becomes painful. Transforming itself into pure suffering.

We learn to love life on the altar of our sacrifice.

A form of love that risks to get ourselves lost forever.

Love is a rainbow of a thousand colors and we have chosen the darkest.

But only corpses don't make mistakes. In our erring, there's always the hope to still be alive.

Ignorant but alive.

There's hope that someday we will understand. One day we will be able to choose the liveliest colors of that marvelous rainbow.

I find myself at the foot of a mountain. My goal is to climb to the top.

But behind me there is the sea. A mysterious force pushes me towards the sea, to plunge myself into its depth.

The water is fresh, inviting. I feel I will be lulled, enveloped in an endless dream.

The flakey rock of the mountain is dry

and sharp. There are no paths to go up. It's tiring to go up the mountain. To immerse yourself into the sea is easy.

I hesitate. I doubt. I lose sight of the goal.

The top.

I take a step towards the sea. I'm attracted towards its immense depth. It's a magnetic force that hypnotizes me. That makes me fall asleep.

A gust of wind wakes me up. It brings me back to myself. I fight the sleepiness. I take my eyes off the sea and set them again towards the mountain. I see the top. I want to go there. It doesn't matter if the way up will be difficult and full of obstacles. It wouldn't be a goal if it were as easy to reach as jumping into the sea.

I want to go up there. I want to see the world from that high perspective. I'll always have time then to jump in the sea.

I go up. The rocks roll under my feet. I stumble, I slow down, and I go again. I gather my courage and reach a good height. I get more trust. I speed up. I think of the goal as if I have already reached it. That thought distracts me when instead the mountain requires all of my concentration. The inevitable happens.

I slip… I fall…

The hand of a gigantic white being, similar to a yeti, grabs hold of me. The astonishing strength of that arm saved me. I just have the time to pull myself together, to get over the fear, when that immense creature has already disappeared. If I had met that creature under other circumstances I would have thought of it as an invincible enemy, as an immoveable obstacle.

Instead, it was the very obstacle that saved me.

I passed a test.

I continue in my ascent and I meet a being of light. He stands apart and says not a word. His silent presence comforts me. His sweet look reassures me. I don't have to be afraid of anything. I'm on the right path.

I make a gesture with my hand to thank him for coming. Then I continue.

I reach the top. A narrow path, carved in the rock, leads me to an opening. A sort of cavern.

I enter.

It's not a cavern. It's a tunnel.

There's no light inside. Only a mysterious electricity that runs through its vault. Without fear, I advance in that dark cavern. A luminescent skull shoots several times above my head.

I quicken my steps, I run… The white light of the exit gets closer. I hold my breath and go through.

Through my goal.

The tunnel opens to an enchanted land. A valley without time. I feel light, able to fly. At the end of the valley, I see an expanse of crystal clear water where strange creatures are drinking.

I smile and think: water, in the end I found you!

I reflect on it. Sea and mountain. Humid and dry. Water and fire. Passive and active.

I reflect and think about the android.

I reflect and think about the little girl.

In his mechanical strength, the android is an invincible warrior. The expression of an exterior principle, male, able to act, to do, to dominate.

The little girl instead, is sensitive, welcoming, receptive… what else could it be if not that feminine that didn't know how to grow in me. That had to hide behind the thick mask of a metallic robot.

Now it all seems clear. But the more I try to convince myself the less I feel I understand.

I decide to look again. This time with a neutral look, detached, scientific.

The android is big. In that there is no doubt. It's powerful, yes, but his power is that of a tank of which they've taken out the motor. Looking at it better now it seems empty.

Its movements, its looking at the world

from the viewer, is a run-down, passive, reactive movement. Without an apparent goal. It's like a gigantic empty cavity of which is missing the propulsive spark. The seed. The project.

Now I understand: he is female!

A female waiting to be made fruitful. This thought brings me an intense emotion. But I want to remain neutral, detached. I want to gather information, not create new illusionary associations.

I turn my eyes towards Jade, the little girl with blond hair and a distant look.

She's searching, but she already knows. She already knows, but she's still searching.

Her little being is anything but passive. Her movements are not casual, but similar to an arrow attracted by its target. In her flight, she searches for the target. But even though she's searching for it, she already knows that she cannot miss it.

She is therefore not Jade, but stem of Jade. She is the member. The impregnating seed. The essence. The motor.

She is male!

Everything is turned upside-down and paradoxically my vision is straightened out. The female is the symbol of the male. The male is the symbol of the female. The form changes but the first and only-begotten substance doesn't change.

That little girl is a little boy!

That little boy never died!

I laugh!

I shout!

I yell!

I rejoice!

Anything is still possible.

A powerful vision opens up to me.

I am at peace. I sit on the edge of a great lake of pure water. I calmly observe its surface. I gaze upon those waters that move smoothly and assume the strangest forms.

My child is alive! As a great mother, I am waiting.

I am waiting to find within me that

dimension of innocence, which I have neglected for far too long. I am waiting to reconnect with my feelings. With the breathing of my belly. I am waiting to bring all of this to my heart. To see my life within new dimensions.

Intensity, essence, joy. Now I can try again to open up my being to those qualities that were taken from me. That I allowed to be taken from me. Because I was unable to comprehend.

On the edge of that lake now I understand. Now that child can live within me again.

Healing.

His eyes have changed. They are the eyes of Jade.

The eyes of the heart.

That look that erased her face, that muffled explosion, did not hit only her look. But distorted also her smile. Annihilated her innocence.

I need to learn to laugh again. To run. To play.

I arise and throw stones into the lake. I make them skip on the mirror of the water. How long has it been? How long has it been since I felt... joy of life?

Then I sit down and remain in silence. The lake transforms into a giant screen in which I see scenes from my past. Fragments of life that reflect back to me.

I see a knight that is fighting to save a people that is decimated by famine. His duty is to conquer new lands to feed his people. I see his toil. His effort. His struggle. His victory.

The scene changes. I see a wise man of which many people are following in procession, to ask counsel.

I see a scientist. A pioneer that chooses to close himself up in silence to not reveal the fruits of his discoveries. Too dangerous for the man childs of that time.

The film ends. I am left with a heavy feeling. Of oppression. And a word: responsibility.

The Divas of that lake come to my help. Feminine entities, sweet and welcoming. Their refreshing voices whisper to me words that I have already heard.

“Responsibility. Don’t become a slave of this word. Don’t feel like the destiny of those people still depends on you. Times have changed. Now you can find the right balance and dedicate a little time to yourself.

The difficult task was for then. Now you can find a way to also think of your child. To play and not only to conquer.

Don't be afraid. We are close to you. We will accompany you at this time of transformation, waiting for something greater to reveal itself.

Let the lightheartedness, the joy, the laughs, the tears, flow directly out of your belly. Let your voice make sounds that it never allowed itself to make before.

We are by your side like colored soap bubbles.

We caress you, giving you a feeling of freshness and rebirth. Don't be afraid. Something else will reveal itself in the future. Something that will give you strength and courage to face great things."

I find myself on my balcony. I look again at the roofs. The chimneys that always smoke and the walls ruined by time.

Time.

Melody from other worlds that invite us to watch with the eagle's eyes. From above. Far away. Or hurl down in a nosedive.

Time. Invincible enemy that blocks the road. That blinds you with its unrelenting arrow, giving you vision of the superior worlds.

The child is with me. In the space of this moment where my soul struggles to survive. Where breathlessly I gather the kaleidoscopical fragments of my existence.

I want to blend them together to produce a magic element, of which I can give the name of…

I.

But my strength fails me. The sight of the eagle blurs. The child that lives in me, under the thin layer of my skin, is again afraid.

The task I am asking him to do is once again too big. So he implores:

"I am not ready to fuse with you. I lack

the strength. I lack the courage. I am afraid to die."

I cry. I cry because only now, for the first time, am I able to catch sight of the face of that frightened child. How can I ask him to be so strong? He is only a child. A child that wants to play. A child that has just learned how to play.

I will wait.

I will give him time.

I understand that we are more like children that will venture into jungles full of danger than real explorers. We deceive ourselves that we know the road. But most of the time we just go around in circles.

Yet we are beings of infinite possibilities. Capable of realizing the greatest that lives in this universe.

The divine abides in us and at the same time we have lost our way home.

If we accept this paradox, if we destroy the false hope that someone else can make the trip in our place, we can find the right measure to grow.

We need to walk alone and at the same time we need someone to illuminate our way. Someone that helps us to not get lost.

In this equilibrium resides the sense of the path of man. The sense of my search and of my battle.

The child sits naked on the humid ground of a luxuriant jungle. His little hands curiously touch that powerful nature. He explores its most secret places. He caresses the mysterious forms. Unaware of the danger that every move hides.

The tiger watches him. Its eyes express the unstoppable strength of the incandescent lava in eruption.

The child asks:

“Who are you?”

The beast replies:

“I am the symbol of strength. Of power. But your likes don’t understand. They believe I am a killer. They don’t understand that I only kill to feed myself. To feed my little ones. To honor my nature.

In my strength I don’t dominate. In my power I don’t judge. In my ferociousness I don’t crush. I simply do that for which I’ve been created for. I don’t have anything to repent of.”

The child asks again:

“Is that good?”

“Yes, that is good.”

Answered the tiger.

"You don't need my claws, my fangs. Only if you will understand the ferocity and anger that live in you will you be able to transform them into strength and energy of life. Only then can the tiger in you be able to transform into a true eagle. Only then can you use your power for other purposes. To reach the highest peaks."

"What do I need to do?"

Again the child asks.

"Don't separate the worlds. Get out of the scheme of good and evil. Of the prey and the hunter. Explore new territories. Draw on true strength. Beyond judgment."

The child blushes and the wild beast roars. Its roar is sweet and smooth. Its solar voice is a delicate rumble.

"Using your power doesn't mean to

renounce the heart. You are the new man. You are the bearer of this new quality.

The strength of the heart.

Use your strength to guard that in which you believe. That which you love. Don't doubt. You will make the world more beautiful. Let the fire that burns in you take its course. Let it reveal itself. Don't be afraid of your beauty.

A child is not ashamed. Who is innocent is not ashamed. Who is in the truth is not ashamed. Remind yourself of this, always."

The tiger went away. The child looks and sees that his chest shines with an indescribable light.

Now he is not a child anymore.

He is a noble warrior.

Strong muscles cover his figure. His naked body is at the same time sweet and terrible.

Loving and invincible.

I find myself crouched down on the ground. On my balcony. I cry endless tears under the pouring rain. Tears that wash my being from the terrible shame.

I want to vomit.

My body rebels. It tries to expel a shapeless mass, foul-smelling, that obstructs the mouth of my stomach.

The mouth of all those judgments that from time unmemorable have poisoned my being.

Nausea and vomit. Then a throbbing pain in my head. The wound of an orgasm of pleasure that my body never gave itself. Never knew how to reach.

I shout!

And with the strength of my desperation I shake off of me a thousand revolting demons that have found a place to live in me. In my soul. Vampires that suck the essence of my life.

The Eros. The joy.

The smoke of a thousand chimneys is nestled in my lungs, preventing my breathing. Preventing me to gather the intense perfumes of life.

But a piercing orgasm has suddenly expelled that black rot.

Once again the breath of existence can feed my fire. Make my flame bright.

Once again everything is possible.

My child is not afraid anymore. He celebrated its death. He won his battle.

His heart is ready to fuse with mine. He's ready to give his essence. To rebirth into a new identity. True. Imperishable…

I.

I am not alone anymore. The mysterious being that discreetly observed my ascent is here with me.

Its voice is a melody that comes from a faraway galaxy. The call from home.

I look and in his eyes I see an infinite

space. Time and space in a single undivided reality.

“You called me. For a long time you have called me and I came. Great was your call. Now the time has come to go up higher. To get in contact with new dimensions. To open the gateway towards other spheres.

Now you are ready. A great explosion will arrive. You can leave the past behind and open up yourself to new understandings.”

I feel new vibrations embracing me. The space of a new movement that takes form in me. I feel immensely thankful. Now all can begin again.

Now, at last, I am reborn.

www.ingramcontent.com/pod-product-compliance
Ingram Content Group UK Ltd.
Pitfield, Milton Keynes, MK11 3LW, UK
UKHW020219250726
13967UKWH00001B/85

9 781446 664261